Thesaurus Rex

Written by Laya Steinberg
Illustrated by Debbie Harter

Barefoot Books
Celebrating Art and Story

Thesaurus Rex drinks his milk:
sip, sup, swallow, swill.

Whoops!
He's had a
messy spill.

foraging,

poking.

Splish, splash, his feet are soaking!

Thesaurus Rex likes to play:

frolic,   rollick,   frisk

and romp.

Wow! He's found a muddy swamp.

Thesaurus Rex starts to slip:

skid,

slither,

Thesaurus Rex lands in mud:
slime, slush, mire and muck.

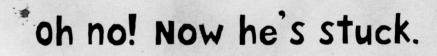

oh no! Now he's stuck.

Thesaurus Rex calls his Mom:
howl,
yowl,
squeal
and shout.

Whoosh, plop!
She pulls him out.

Thesaurus Rex must get clean:

wash,

bathe,

Thesaurus Rex is ready to eat:
munch, crunch, nibble, gnaw.

Chomp!
He likes his
dinner raw.

springs

and flies.

Tomorrow holds a new surprise.

Thesaurus Rex is all wrapped up:
bundled,
    covered,
        tucked in tight.

He'll have happy dreams tonight. Goodnight!

Barefoot Books
3 Bow Street, 3rd Floor
Cambridge, MA 02138

This book was typeset in Bokka.
The illustrations were prepared in watercolor, pen and ink and crayon on thick watercolor paper

Graphic design by Big Blu Ltd,
Color separation by Grafiscan, Italy
Printed and bound in Hong Kong by South China Printing Co.
This book has been printed on 100% acid-free paper

1 3 5 7 9 8 6 4 2

Publisher Cataloging-in-Publication Data (U.S.)

Steinberg, Laya.
    Thesaurus Rex / written by Laya Steinberg ; illustrated
by Debbie Harter. — 1st ed.
[24] p. : col. ill. ; cm.
Summary: Thesaurus Rex, a loveable dinosaur, introduces
children to synonyms in this rhyming text that takes him
throughout his day.
ISBN 1-84148-042-8
1. English Language — Synonyms and antonyms—Juvenile
Literature. (1. English Language—Synonyms and antonyms.)
I. Harter, Debbie. II. Title.
428.1 [E] 21   PE1591.S84 2003

To Bruce, Marina and Perry, my devoted family, who I love, adore, cherish and treasure — L. S.

For Finlay — D. H.